PEANUTS®
Gobble Up, SNOOPY!

by Charles M. Schulz
adapted by May Nakamura
illustrated by Scott Jeralds

Ready-to-Read

Simon Spotlight
New York London Toronto Sydney New Delhi

SIMON SPOTLIGHT
An imprint of Simon & Schuster Children's Publishing Division
1230 Avenue of the Americas, New York, New York 10020
This Simon Spotlight edition September 2019
© 2019 Peanuts Worldwide LLC
All rights reserved, including the right of reproduction in whole or in part in any form. SIMON SPOTLIGHT,
READY-TO-READ, and colophon are registered trademarks of Simon & Schuster, Inc. For information about
special discounts for bulk purchases, please contact Simon & Schuster Special Sales at 1-866-506-1949 or
business@simonandschuster.com.
Manufactured in the United States of America 0719 LAK
2 4 6 8 10 9 7 5 3 1
ISBN 978-1-5344-4861-2 (hc)
ISBN 978-1-5344-4860-5 (pbk)
ISBN 978-1-5344-4862-9 (eBook)

Charlie Brown is sitting outside when his sister, Sally, walks by with an envelope.
"What is that?" he asks.

"I wrote a thank-you letter
to Linus," Sally replies.
"It says I'm thankful that
he is my Sweet Babboo!"

Snoopy likes the idea
of writing a thank-you letter.
He doesn't have a "Sweet Babboo,"
but he knows exactly
who he wants to thank.

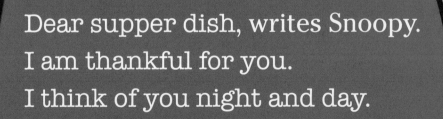

Dear supper dish, writes Snoopy.
I am thankful for you.
I think of you night and day.

You are more precious to me
than anything in the world.

You are always there for me,
in the rain and in the snow.

We have been through
a lot together,
continues Snoopy.
Do you remember when I took you
to a baseball game?

You helped me catch the ball in the ninth inning!

Do you remember the day we were
almost late for supper?
writes Snoopy.

You let me ride you like a sled
so we could get home in time!

The best part, of course,
is the food we have shared
together.
Hot dogs, popcorn,
doughnuts, dog food,
and my favorite . . .
doggie treats!

Thank you for being such
a good pal to share a meal with.
Your friend,
Snoopy

Writing this letter has made Snoopy
very hungry.
Is it suppertime yet?
he wonders.

Charlie Brown usually brings
meals for Snoopy, but Snoopy
wants supper early.
He hits the supper dish
with a bone to try to get
Charlie Brown's attention.

It rings like a gong,
but there is no sign
of Charlie Brown.

Next, Snoopy walks up to the house
and does his suppertime dance.

He twirls, wiggles, and boogies . . .
but there is no sign
of Charlie Brown.

Then Snoopy tries to send signals from his mind. He wiggles his paws and thinks, *Back door, open! Supper, come out!*

The back door does not open,
and there is no sign
of Charlie Brown.

Snoopy is getting hungrier.
Finally, he bangs on the back door
with his foot.

Charlie Brown opens the door.
"It is not suppertime yet!"
he yells, and he slams the door.

Snoopy sighs and returns
to his doghouse.
He waits, and waits, and waits.

A back door never opens when it is being watched, he thinks.

When Snoopy is about to give up,
the back door finally opens.
"Time for food,"
Charlie Brown says.
"Come inside, and bring your
supper dish!"

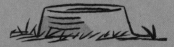

Inside? Snoopy wonders.
He does not eat inside
very often.

When Snoopy walks in,
Charlie Brown says,
"Surprise! Thank you for being
our favorite beagle.
We planned a feast just for you!"

The table is filled with Snoopy's
favorite foods and more!
There are sandwiches, doughnuts,
popcorn, dog food, hot dogs,
and dog treats, of course!

All of Snoopy's friends are there.
They do their own suppertime dances!

Snoopy is so happy.
He gets to eat his favorite foods
with his friends!

Then Snoopy realizes that
he wants to write another
thank-you letter.

He forgot to thank someone
who is very, very important.
It is his favorite person!

The letter will begin,
Dear Round-Headed Kid,
Thank you for supplying me with
my supper dish!

First, though, it is suppertime—
time to gobble up his supper
and enjoy a meal with friends!